Jen's Best Gift Ever

Written by
Laura Appleton-Smith

Illustrated by
Keinyo White

Laura Appleton-Smith was born and raised in Vermont and holds a degree in English from Middlebury College. Laura is a primary school teacher who has combined her talents in creative writing and her experience in early childhood education to create *Books to Remember*. Laura lives in New Hampshire with her husband, Terry. This is her third book from Flyleaf Publishing.

Keinyo White is a graduate of the Rhode Island School of Design with a B.F.A. in illustration. He currently produces children's books and freelance illustrations from his studio in Los Angeles.

A Book to Remember™
Published by Flyleaf Publishing

For orders or information, contact us at **(800) 449-7006**.
Please visit our website at **www.flyleafpublishing.com**

Fourth Edition 9/16
Library of Congress Catalog Card Number: 98-96630
ISBN-13: 978-0-9658246-9-9
Printed and bound in the USA at Worzalla Publishing, Stevens Point, WI

To LAS for her unwavering faith and patience,
and for my wife.

KW

For Bailey.

LAS

It is six o'clock and the sun is just up.

Jen lifts back her quilt and jumps from bed.

She runs to the calendar next to her desk.
At last, it is Jen's birthday!

"I am seven–seven, seven, seven," she sings
as she runs to tell Mom and Dad.

Just as Jen gets to Mom and Dad's bed she stops…

On the rug next to the bed is a gift box.
It has a big ribbon on the top.

"Happy Birthday, Jen," sing Mom and Dad and Jen's sister Emma.

They tell Jen to lift the lid from the box.

She lifts the lid…

In the box, snug in a soft blanket, is a black kitten.

Jen lifts the kitten up.

"What will I name him?" she asks.

Just then the kitten jumps from Jen's hands.

He lands on the rug and runs under Mom and Dad's bed.

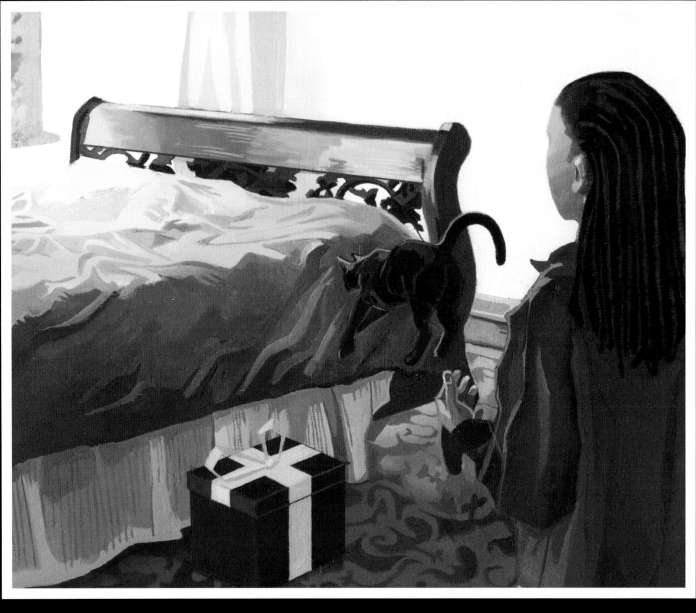

The kitten is hidden under the bed and Jen cannot get him out.

Jen has a plan.

She pulls a strand of ribbon from the gift box.

Jen drags the ribbon on the rug next to the bed.

The kitten runs out and snags the ribbon.
He jumps and twists and flips as he runs after it.

"I will name him Frolic," Jen tells Emma.

"Frolic is the best name for a kitten that can
run and jump so well."

Frolic runs and jumps and flips and spins
until he has to rest. Jen lifts him onto her lap.

She thanks Mom and Dad.

A kitten is the best gift Jen has ever had.

Prerequisite Skills

Single consonants and short vowels
Final double consonants **ff**, **gg**, **ll**, **nn**, **ss**, **tt**, **zz**
Consonant /k/ **ck**
Consonant digraphs /ng/ **ng**, **n[k]**, /th/ **th**, /hw/ **wh**
Schwa /ə/ **a**, **e**, **i**, **o**, **u**
Long /ē/ **ee**, **y**
r-Controlled /ûr/ **er**
Variant vowel /aw/ **al**, **all**
Consonant /l/ **le**
/d/ or /t/ **-ed**

Prerequisite Skills are foundational phonics skills
that have been previously introduced.

Target Letter-Sound Correspondence is
the letter-sound correspondence introduced
in the story.

High-Frequency Puzzle Words are
high-frequency irregular words.

Story Puzzle Words are irregular words
that are not high frequency.

Decodable Words are words that can be
decoded solely on the basis of the letter-sound
correspondences or phonetic elements that
have been introduced.

Target Letter-Sound Correspondence

Foundational Skills
Consolidation

Story Puzzle Words

birthday	name
calendar	onto

High-Frequency Puzzle Words

for	she
from	so
he	they
of	to
out	what
pulls	

Decodable Words

a	cannot	has	lap	runs	thanks
after	Dad	her	last	seven	that
am	Dad's	hidden	lid	sing	the
and	desk	him	lift	sings	then
as	drags	I	lifts	sister	top
asks	Emma	in	mom	six	twists
at	ever	is	next	snags	under
back	flips	it	o'clock	snug	until
bed	frolic	Jen	on	soft	up
best	get	Jen's	plan	spins	well
big	gets	jump	quilt	stops	will
black	gift	jumps	rest	strand	
blanket	had	just	ribbon	sun	
box	hands	kitten	rug	tell	
can	happy	lands	run	tells	